Freshwater Fish

TEXT BY ELAINE PASCOE

PHOTOGRAPHS BY DWIGHT KUHN

BLACKBIRCH PRESS

An imprint of Thomson Gale, a part of The Thomson Corporation

THOMSON

GALE

Detroit • New York • San Francisco • San Diego • New Haven, Conn. • Waterville, Maine • London • Munich

For more information, contact
Blackbirch Press
27500 Drake Rd.
Farmington Hills, MI 48331-3535
Or you can visit our Internet site at http://www.gale.com

Photo Credits: All pages © Dwight R. Kuhn Photography
              © Dave Kuhn / Dwight R. Kuhn Photography — p. 6, p. 47

LIBRARY OF CONGRESS CATALOGING-IN-PUBLICATION DATA

Pascoe, Elaine.
  Freshwater Fish / by Elaine Pascoe ; photographs by Dwight Kuhn.
    p. cm. — (Nature close-up)
  Includes index.
  ISBN 1-4103-0308-X (alk. paper)
  1. Fish-freshwater—Juvenile literature. I. Kuhn, Dwight. II. Title III. Series: Pascoe,
Elaine. Nature close-up.

Printed in China
10 9 8 7 6 5 4 3 2 1

Contents

1 Sleek Swimmers   **4**

   Built for Water   6

   Inside Story   11

   Senses   14

   Fish Food   17

   Fish Fry   19

   Fish and People   24

2 Keeping and Caring for Freshwater Fish   **26**

   A Simple Aquarium for Bettas   28

   An Aquarium for Tropical Fish   30

   Adding Fish   32

   Feeding and Care   34

3 Investigating Freshwater Fish   **36**

   Will Fish Swim Toward or Away from Light?   37

   Does a Male Betta Prefer to Build Its Nest Under Cover or in the Open?   38

   How Do Male Bettas Behave Toward Each Other?   40

   What Kinds of Food Do Your Aquarium Fish Prefer?   41

   More Activities with Freshwater Fish   43

   Results and Conclusions   44

Some Words About Freshwater Fish   **46**

For More Information   **47**

Index   **48**

1

Sleek Swimmers

With a flash of silver, a fish leaps to catch a fly. It breaks the smooth surface of a pond with a splash, and then it's gone. Ripples spread out across the pond surface. In a minute everything is still again. Except for that brief glimpse, you might never know that the pond is full of fish.

Fish live in every kind of water, from small streams to the oceans that cover 70 percent of earth's surface. They are fascinating creatures, perfectly designed for their watery world. Fish range in size from the dwarf goby, which is no bigger than a pencil eraser, to the whale shark. The whale shark can grow as long as two school buses and weigh more than two elephants.

Many kinds of freshwater fish, like this goldfish, can be kept in home aquariums.

Like most fish, the peacock cichlid is shaped like a little torpedo.

The dwarf goby and the whale shark are both ocean fishes. This book is mostly about freshwater fishes—those that live in lakes, rivers, streams, and ponds. Less than 1 percent of the world's water is fresh. But freshwater fishes make up more than 40 percent of the thousands of fish species that live on earth.

Built for Water

Fish can be long or short, skinny or broad. But most fish share a basic body plan. That plan is designed for life in the water.

6

Living in water has special challenges. For one thing, water is denser than air. Thus it is more difficult to move through water than through air. If you go swimming, you know that it takes much more energy to swim than to walk the same distance. But most fish are streamlined, to make movement through the water easier. The basic fish shape is smooth and sleek, so it slices through the water like a torpedo.

The pumpkinseed sunfish is found in North American lakes and streams.

7

Fish move through the water with the help of their fins. Fish fins can be stumpy, spiky, or winglike. Most fish have rayed fins, which are stiffened with spines. The fins are set along the fish's back and underside and in pairs on its side. Each fin has a job.

The tail fin, or caudal fin, is the main motor for most fish. The fish wiggles its body from side to side. As it does, the tail fin sweeps through the water, pushing the fish forward. Back fins, or dorsal fins, help keep the fish upright in the water. The anal fin, on the fish's underside, helps keep it upright too. Most fish have two pairs of side fins, called pectoral and pelvic fins. They help the fish make sharp turns and fast stops.

The male betta has brilliant coloring and long, elegant fins.

A fish's skin is covered with mucus. Special cells in the skin produce this slimy coating. It protects the fish from diseases. And by making the skin super smooth, it helps the fish zip through the water. Most fish also have a protective outer layer of scales. These thin plates are almost like a suit of armor for some types of fish. But other types of fish have small or soft scales.

Fish scales are transparent and colorless. A fish's color is in its skin, in special **pigment** cells. Fish come in every color you can imagine, from brilliant blues, reds, and yellows to drab browns. Many tropical fish have bold stripes and patterns. Others are colored to blend in with their surroundings. This helps them hide from prey—and from predators that might want to eat them.

The male betta's scales are transparent. They let the bright color of the skin below show through.

Many fish can change their colors. The pigments in their skin cells can spread or shrink in response to signals from the nervous system. This causes areas of color to grow larger or smaller. Fish change color to match their surroundings, to attract mates, or to threaten enemies.

During courtship, a male three-spined stickleback's eyes turn light blue, and his underside turns red.

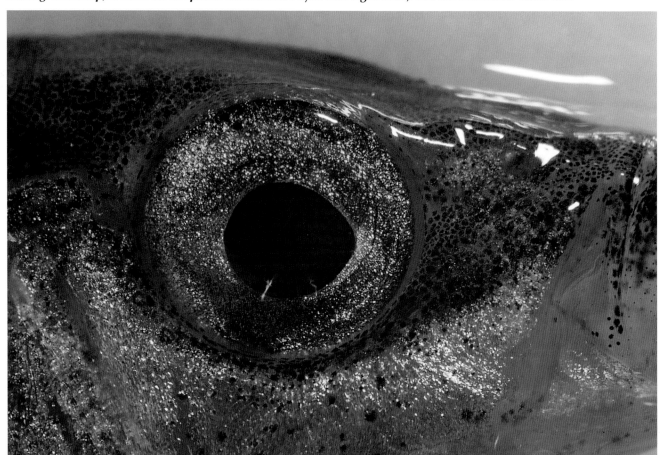

Inside Story

Like you, a fish has a skeleton inside its body. In most fish the skeleton is made of bone. A few kinds of fish, including sharks, have skeletons made of **cartilage**. This is the same flexible material that gives shape to your ears and the tip of your nose.

A fish also has a **spinal cord**, a long bundle of nerves running down the back. The spinal cord connects the fish's brain to the rest of its body. A row of bones called vertebrae protects the spinal cord and forms the fish's backbone. This makes fish, like people, **vertebrates**.

Unlike people, however, fish are **cold-blooded**. This means that a fish's body temperature depends on the temperature of the water around it. If the temperature drops or rises too far, the fish may die.

Fish need oxygen to live. To get it, they breathe water. Instead of lungs, they have special organs called **gills** that pull oxygen from the water. In most fish the gills are placed on each side of the head and protected by gill covers. The gills are made up of tiny threads of tissue filled with blood vessels.

The pacu is a tropical freshwater fish. Some kinds of pacus can grow more than 2 feet (61 cm) long.

11

The dark line behind this betta's head marks the edge of its gill cover.

To breathe, the fish closes its gill covers and takes in water through its mouth. Then it closes its mouth, opens the gill covers, and pumps the water out through the gills. Oxygen passes from the water to the blood vessels in the gills. Carbon dioxide and other waste gases pass from the blood to the water.

Most fish die if they are out of water. Their gills collapse and dry out. But some fish can get oxygen by gulping air through their mouths. These fish live in murky swamps and other places where there is not much oxygen in the water. They come to the surface to breathe.

A fish's heart has two chambers. One chamber pumps blood out to the gills and to the rest of the body. The blood delivers oxygen and nutrients and picks up wastes. The heart's second chamber collects the blood on its return trip.

A fish's body is heavier than water. Why doesn't the fish sink to the bottom? Some fish stay afloat by swimming nonstop. But most fish have a special organ that lets them hang in the water with no effort at all. It's called a swim bladder. The swim bladder is a gas-filled pouch, like a little balloon, located above the stomach. The amount of gas in the bladder adjusts to help the fish rise, sink, or hover at one depth in the water.

WHY SALMON LEAVE HOME

Most freshwater fish cannot live in the ocean. And most ocean fish cannot survive in freshwater. But a few kinds of fish can move back and forth between salt water and freshwater. Among them are salmon.

Salmon hatch from eggs in freshwater streams. When the young fish are a year or two old, they swim hundreds of miles downriver to the sea. They spend two years or more in the ocean, feeding and growing fat. Then they return to fresh water to spawn.

Many salmon go back to the exact streams where they were born. It can be quite a struggle for the fish to swim upstream against the current. But the salmons' instinct to return is strong. They leap through rapids and other obstacles.

A salmon makes its way upstream toward its spawning ground.

Senses

Like people, fish see, hear, smell, taste, and feel the world around them. But fish senses are designed for underwater life. And fish have some senses that people do not have.

Fish have two eyes, in most cases one on each side of the head. This gives a fish a wide view of its world. It can look up, down, forward, and back. Its only blind spots are directly behind and below its body. Many fish can rotate their eyes independently. They can look up and down at the same time.

With eyes on both sides of its head, this stickleback can see in all directions.

Fish have no tears, and their eyes are always open. Living in water, they do not need tears to moisten their eyes or lids to protect them from strong light. But they cannot see very far through water. Fish that live in dark or murky water rely on other senses. Catfish feel their way with sensitive whiskers called **barbels**, for example.

Fish are very sensitive to touch. And even fish that live in clear water rely on their sense of smell. Smell helps them find food and mates. Fish have two smell pouches, one on each side of the head. The pouches are lined with special cells that detect odors in the water. Each pouch has two nostrils. Water flows in one nostril and out the other.

In water, sounds travel faster than they do through air. Most fish have excellent hearing. They have two ears, one on each side of the head. The ears are located inside the body, so they are not visible. The ears are also the fish's balance organs. They tell the fish which way its body is pointed in the water.

A catfish feels its way with sensitive whiskers called barbels.

In water, sounds and movements create tiny changes in water pressure. These changes, or vibrations, travel long distances. Fish have a special system that can sense the changes. This helps them find prey and warns them when predators are near.

The system is called the lateral line system. It is made up of mucus-filled tubes that run down each side of the fish's body, just under the skin. Small pores mark the line on the skin. Vibrations in the water set off vibrations in the tubes. That triggers nerve signals that alert the fish.

Fish can even use their lateral lines to navigate. As the fish swims, it creates its own vibrations. These vibrations bounce off nearby objects. The lateral lines sense the echoes, and the fish avoids the objects.

Some fish use electricity to navigate and find prey. They include electric eels, electric catfish, knifefish, and a few others. These fish have special organs that produce a field of electricity as they swim. If another fish enters the field, the electric fish senses it. Electric eels can send out a powerful shock to stun their prey.

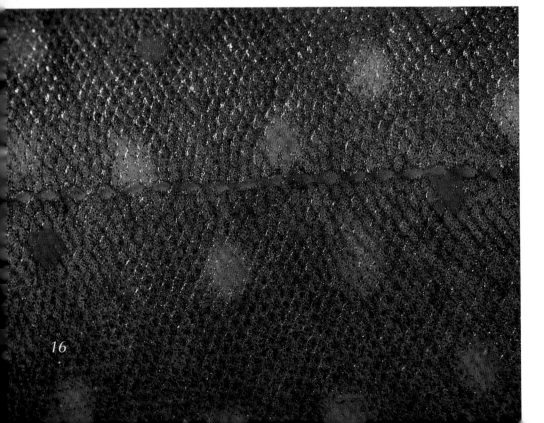

A line of small pores on the side of a brook trout marks the location of the fish's lateral line system.

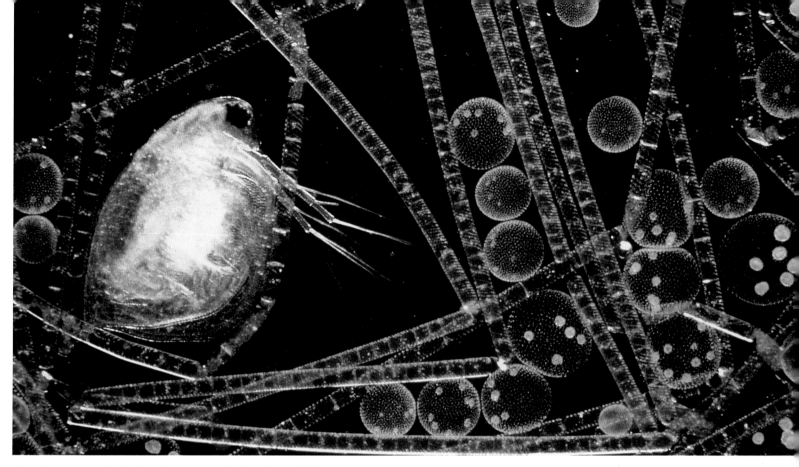

The tiny water flea is food for many kinds of small fish.

Fish Food

Fish spend most of their time swimming around looking for food. They eat lots of different things. Some eat mainly plants. Some are **scavengers** that scour the bottoms of lakes and ponds, eating wastes and dead material. They help keep the water clean. Many fish are predators—they catch and eat other animals. Small predator fish eat water fleas and other tiny creatures. Larger fish eat insects, worms—and other fish.

A fish's teeth may be on its jaws, on its tongue, or even in its throat, depending on the fish and the kind of food it eats. For example, pike are fierce freshwater predators. They have strong jaws lined with sharp teeth that catch and tear prey. Carp are scavengers that also feed on small insects. A carp has no teeth in its mouth. Instead, it has teeth in its throat for grinding up its food.

Many fish eat insects, such as this damselfly nymph.

A male betta builds a nest of air bubbles. After spawning, it will hold the fertilized eggs.

Fish Fry

Every kind of fish mates and produces young in its own time and way. But the basic steps are the same. In most species, females release their **eggs** into the water. The male fish then release their sperm. This is called spawning. The water brings the eggs and **sperm** together, so **fertilization** takes place. The eggs then develop, and young fish, or **fry**, hatch in the water.

Some fish make nests for their eggs. The male betta builds a nest of bubbles near the water surface. The male gulps air at the surface to make the bubbles. The bubbles are covered with sticky mucus, so they do not pop and are held together as they float.

WHY FISH GO TO SCHOOL

A male stickleback prods a female to prompt her to lay eggs.

Many fish band together in big groups called schools. Members of a school are all the same type of fish and about the same size. There is no leader in a fish school. But all the fish act together. They swim and turn together, as if they were one animal.

Schooling helps protect members from predators. A predator may snap up one or two fish in a school, but the rest will get away safely. Schooling also makes it easy to find a mate. And some fish feed in schools. Piranhas, which live in South American rivers, can kill large animals by ganging up in schools.

The male stickleback courts the female by showing her the fine nest he has built. He prompts her to lay eggs by prodding her tail. After the eggs are fertilized, he guards the eggs from predators. And he fans the water over the eggs with his fins, to keep them supplied with oxygen.

Stickleback young hatch from eggs in the nest.

The guppy is one of the few fish that give birth to live young.

Mollies, guppies, and some other fish give birth to live young. Males and females mate, so the eggs are fertilized and develop in the female's body.

Most young fish are on their own as soon as they are born. Only a few kinds of fish care for their young. Larger fish and other predators quickly snap up many fry. Giant water bugs, diving birds, and animals like otters, raccoons, and shrews all catch fish. But fish produce so many young that some always survive to become adults.

A school of female sticklebacks.

23

Fish and People

Fishing is a sport and an industry. Trout, sunfish, and catfish are among the fish that sport fishers take from streams and lakes. In the ocean, commercial fishing boats use nets to catch huge numbers of fish.

Fish are a major source of food for people. A fifth of the protein people consume worldwide comes from fish, especially ocean fish. Today this food source is in danger, though. **Overfishing** has seriously cut the numbers of some fish. People have created other problems for fish. Water pollution has hurt fish in many places. People have drained wetlands, which are important as nurseries for many fish species.

Fish have an important place in the food chain. But people enjoy just watching fish, too. An aquarium is a fascinating window on the underwater world.

The brook trout, found in freshwater streams, is a popular game fish.

2

Keeping and Caring for Freshwater Fish

A home aquarium can let you watch fish close-up and learn about their fascinating behaviors. In this chapter, you'll find tips for setting up a basic aquarium and keeping some kinds of freshwater tropical fish.

You can buy fish and the supplies you need at a pet or aquarium store. The staff in many stores can provide expert advice, too. There are also many excellent books on this subject, and some are listed on page 47.

Remember that to thrive, fish need the right conditions. Keep fish if you're ready to set up a proper aquarium and maintain it, with regular cleaning and other care. If you give them the conditions they need, your fish will reward you with hours of enjoyment.

- Clear glass bowl, at least
  1 quart (1 liter)
- Betta
- Betta food
- Optional: clean aquarium
  gravel, aquarium plants

A Simple Aquarium for Bettas

Male bettas, also called Siamese fighting fish, are especially beautiful. They are also easy to keep and can live happily in a simple, small container. Bettas do not need a lot of oxygen in the water because they can get extra oxygen from air. They do this with an organ called a labyrinth, next to their gills. The fish go to the surface and gulp air to fill the labyrinth.

You can buy bettas and other supplies at a pet store.

What to Do:

1. Set up the bowl before you buy your fish. Most tap water has been treated with chlorine, which will harm fish.

28

2. Put water in the bowl and then let it stand for at least 24 hours. "Aging" the water this way will get rid of the chlorine. You can also use a water conditioner sold at pet stores to take the chlorine out immediately. The water should be at room temperature.

3. If you want to use aquarium gravel, rinse it in a strainer and put it in the bottom of the bowl. Add a few live aquarium plants if you want. Just tuck the roots into the gravel.

4. When you bring your betta home, it will be in a plastic container. If you just dump it into its new home, the change in temperature could shock the fish. Instead, put the whole plastic container in the betta bowl and let it sit there for 15 minutes. The temperature in the two containers will even out. Then slowly tear the plastic container and let the fish swim into the bowl.

5. Put only one male betta in a bowl. These fish will fight if they are put together.

6. Keep the bowl in a warm room. If you have a plant in the bowl, it will need bright light. But do not put the bowl in direct sunlight, which could overheat the water.

7. Feed your betta once a day using betta food from the pet store. Give the fish only as much food as it can finish in a few minutes. Uneaten food will foul the water, and overfeeding can make the fish sick.

8. The betta will produce wastes, so you'll need to change the water in the bowl often. A 1-quart (1-liter) bowl will need fresh water at least once a week. Always use water that has been aged for 24 hours or treated to remove chlorine. Make sure the new water is the same temperature as the old water.

What You Need:

- Aquarium [10 gallons (38 liters) or more] with a cover and light
- Aquarium heater
- Thermometer for checking water temperature
- Aquarium filter and filter cartridge
- Clean aquarium gravel
- Live aquarium plants
- Water conditioning chemical
- Optional: Aquarium stand, scrapers or brushes to clean the tank, bucket and siphon for changing water and cleaning gravel, fish net, decorations

An Aquarium for Tropical Fish

You can keep a variety of tropical fish together in an aquarium. The key is to choose types of fish that get along and thrive in the same conditions. This type of aquarium also calls for more equipment than a betta bowl. Guide books, pet-store staff, and other fish hobbyists are all good sources of advice about setting up and stocking an aquarium. This section will cover the basics.

What to Do:

1. Set up the aquarium before you buy the fish. First, test the aquarium to be sure it does not leak. Put the aquarium in the bathtub, fill it, and check for leaks.

2. Place the tank where you want it before you fill it. Pick a place where it will not be knocked over. Make sure it has a sturdy support. Once it is full, it will be very heavy.

3. Rinse the gravel in a strainer. Do not use any soap or detergents. Then spread the cleaned gravel over the bottom of the tank. Place your decorations, if you have any.

4. Put a saucer or other small container on the gravel. Then gently pour room-temperature water onto the saucer. This will keep the water from moving the gravel or stirring up any dirt. Add water until the tank is about one-third full.

5. Place your plants in the tank. Push the plant roots gently down into the gravel. Add a clean stone at the plant base to hold it in place.

6. Slowly add more water until the tank is three-fourths full.

Top: Add water by pouring into a container.
Bottom: Anchor water plants in the gravel.

31

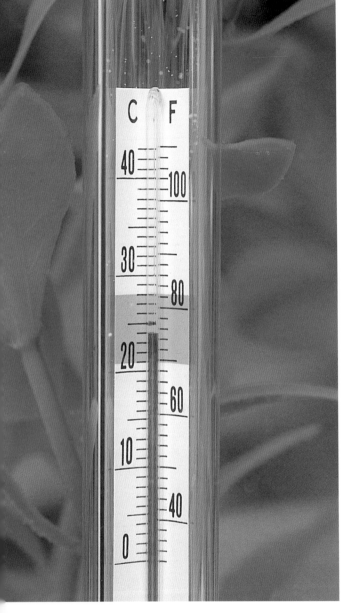

Water should be about 75 degrees F (24 degrees C).

7. Set up the thermometer, heater, and filter. This equipment varies, so follow the directions that come with yours. Ask an adult to help you with the setup.
8. Add warm or cold water to adjust the temperature to about 75 degrees F (24 degrees C).
9. Add the water conditioner according to directions.
10. Cover the tank and turn on the light. The light should be on for 12 to 14 hours a day, for the plants as well as the fish.
11. Do not add fish yet. Wait until the filter makes the water perfectly clear and the temperature stays at about 75 degrees F (24 degrees C). Keep making adjustments to the heater until the temperature holds steady.

Adding Fish

Some fish are more delicate than others. Some are fighters that can cause trouble in a tank. Start with fish that are hardy and easy to keep. These include zebra danios, platies, tetras, gouramis, and cory catfish. There are many other choices, and your pet shop can offer advice. Goldfish do not belong in a mixed tropical fish tank. They like cooler water, and they grow too big. But goldfish are fun to keep in a tank of their own.

Do not buy too many fish. If your tank is overcrowded, the fish will die. One rule of thumb is to have no more than 1 inch (2.5 cm) of fish for each gallon (3.8 liters) of water. This means that in a 10-gallon (38-liter) tank, you have room for five 2-inch (5-cm) fish.

Add fish to your aquarium a few at a time, rather than all at once. This gives the water a chance to adjust. For each new addition, put the plastic container with the fish still sealed inside into the tank. Let the container sit for about 15 minutes while the temperature of the water evens out. Then gently open the container and let the fish swim out into their new home.

Let the plastic bag with fish sit in the water for 15 minutes before opening the bag.

Feeding and Care

Buy fish food that is made for your type of fish. Feed once a day, and give only as much food as the fish can eat in a short time. They should be able to finish flake food before it falls halfway down to the bottom of the tank. Uneaten food will foul the water. And some fish will overeat until they are sick.

Regular water changes will help keep your fish healthy. You do not need to change all the water at once. Plan to replace about a third of the water in the tank every couple of weeks. You can scoop out the old water and then add new water. Make sure the new water is the same temperature and has been treated with water conditioner. If you have a water siphon, you can take water out and clean the gravel at the same time.

Keeping fish is a great hobby, and there is a lot to know about it. You can learn more by reading some of the many books on aquarium fish.

3

Investigating Freshwater Fish

You can learn a lot about fish just by watching how they behave in their tank. In this section, you'll find projects and activities that will help you learn more. Some of the projects can be done with bettas, and others can be done with any aquarium fish.

Will Fish Swim Toward or Away from Light?

In the wild, fish seldom see bright light—just sunlight filtered through water. How do you think they will react to a bright light? Make your best guess, and then do this activity to find out. You can use any aquarium fish.

What to Do:

1. Darken the room by pulling shades and turning off lights. Then turn off the overhead aquarium light for this experiment.
2. Place a flashlight or desk lamp at the side of the aquarium. Turn it on, with the beam pointing into the tank. Watch the fish to see what they do.
3. Turn the light off and move it to the other side of the tank. Then turn it on again, and watch the fish.

Results: What did the fish do? If you have several kinds of fish in the tank, did they all behave the same? Did you get the same results on both sides of the tank?

Conclusion: Based on your results, do you think fish are attracted to light?

What You Need:
- Aquarium with fish
- Strong flashlight or desk lamp

37

What You Need:

- Male betta in container. A rectangular container works better than a round bowl for this activity.
- Plant or plastic cover

Does a Male Betta Prefer to Build Its Nest Under Cover or in the Open?

In the wild, male bettas make nests of bubbles near the water surface. After the female lays her eggs, he fertilizes them and places them in the nest. He guards and cares for the eggs until they hatch.

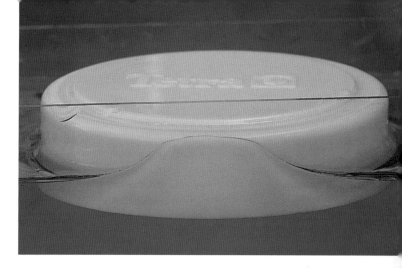

Would a male betta rather build his nest in the open, or in the shelter of a plant or some other cover? Decide what you think, and then do this activity.

What to Do:

1. The betta must be making bubble nests for you to do this experiment. Sometimes you can encourage nest building by putting two males near each other, in separate containers.
2. Float a water plant or plastic cover on one side of the tank. Leave the other side open.

Results: Watch to see if the fish builds its nest under cover or in the open.

Conclusion: What do your results tell you about the kinds of nest sites bettas prefer? What advantages do those sites have for the fish?

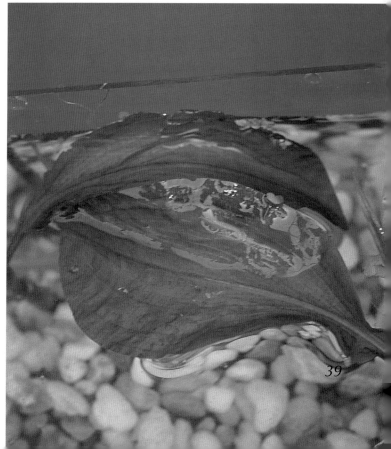

How Do Male Bettas Behave Toward Each Other?

How do you think male bettas will behave if they are in separate containers, placed right next to each other? Will they swim toward or away from each other? Make your best guess based on what you have read about these fish, and then do this activity to see if you are right.

What You Need:
- Two male bettas in separate bowls
- Sheet of cardboard

What to Do:
1. Put the betta bowls next to each other.
2. Watch the fish for a few minutes. See how they behave and what parts of their containers they swim in. Take notes describing what you see.
3. Put a sheet of cardboard between the bowls, so the fish cannot see each other. Watch their behavior and note any changes.

Results: Where did the bettas spend most of their time when they could see each other? Did their swimming patterns or other behavior change when they could not see each other?

Conclusion: Do male bettas see each other as friends or foes? How does the fish's behavior help it in the wild?

If you have only one betta, try placing a mirror next to the bowl. See what the fish does when it sees its reflection.

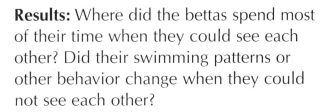

What Kinds of Food Do Your Aquarium Fish Prefer?

Pet stores sell lots of different fish foods. Most of them are not foods that fish find in the wild. Do your fish care what sort of food they get? Decide what you think. Then enlist a helper or two and test your guess with this experiment.

What to Do:

1. Have each person (including yourself) take a bit of a different food in each hand. Be sure that, altogether, you do not give the fish more food than they normally get.
2. Release all the different foods into the tank at the same time.
3. Watch the fish to see what they eat. After a few minutes, remove as much of any uneaten food as you can.

4. Repeat the experiment on other days. Each time, change positions with your helpers, so that the foods are released in different parts of the tank.

Results: Note which foods the fish eat first, and which they do not eat. Make a chart or table that shows your results.

Conclusion: Look for patterns in your results. Do the fish always go for the same type of food? Do different fish prefer different foods?

More Activities with Freshwater Fish

1. Train your fish to come to the surface to be fed. Turn the aquarium light off and on quickly, and then put in the food. Do this every time you feed the fish. Eventually they will swim to the surface as soon as you flick the light on and off.

This type of training is called conditioning. You can use the same method with other signals, such as a noise. See how long it takes the fish to learn this trick.

2. Time your betta's breathing. Keep track of how often the fish comes to the surface for air over a 10-minute period.

3. Draw your fish and label its parts. See if you can identify: nostril, gill cover, pectoral fin, pelvic fin, dorsal fin, anal fin, caudal fin, lateral line.

Results and Conclusions

Here are some possible results and conclusions for the activities on pages 36 to 42. Many factors may affect the results of these activities. If your results differ, try to think of reasons why. Repeat the activity with different conditions, and see if your results change.

Will fish swim toward or away from light?
Your results may vary. Some fish may be startled by sudden changes in light. Many fish are attracted to light, however.

Does a male betta prefer to build its nest under cover or in the open?
Bettas usually build nests under cover, if given the choice.

How do male bettas behave toward each other?
If two male bettas are in the same tank, they will fight. If they are in separate tanks but can see each other, they will spend most of their time threatening each other. They do this by stretching their fins, flaring their gills, and deepening and changing their colors. In the wild, males probably fight to keep other males out of their nesting area. In a tank, male bettas should not see a mirror or other males for more than 20 minutes or so per day. More time can be stressful for the fish.

What kinds of food do your aquarium fish prefer?
Your results will vary depending on the kind of fish you have and what they are used to eating.

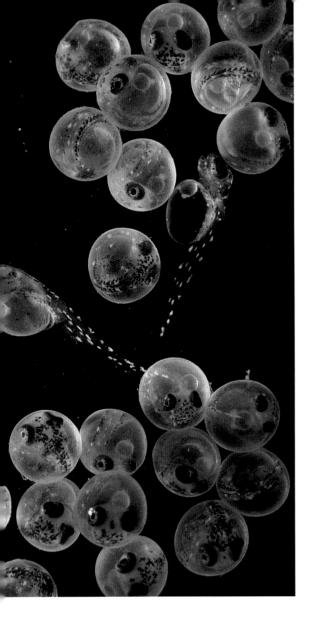

Some Words About Freshwater Fish

barbels Whiskerlike organs that some fish use to feel and taste.

cartilage Flexible material that forms the skeletons of certain fish.

cold-blooded Having a body temperature that changes with the surrounding temperature.

fertilization The joining of egg and sperm.

fry Newly hatched fish.

gills Organs that draw oxygen from water.

nutrients Substances that living things need to live and grow.

overfishing Taking too many fish, so that fish populations shrink.

pigment A chemical that produces color.

scavengers Animals that eat wastes and dead materials.

spinal cord A bundle of nerves that carries signals from the brain to the rest of the body.

vertebrates Animals with a backbone and an internal skeleton.

For More Information

Books

David E. Boruchowitz, *The Simple Guide to Fresh Water Aquariums.* Neptune City, NJ: TFH, 2001.

Mark Evans and Roger A. Caras, *Fish: Pet Care Guides for Kids (ASPCA Pet Care Guide).* London, UK: Dorling Kindersley, 2001.

Mic and Maddy Haargrove, *The Betta: An Owner's Guide to a Happy Healthy Fish.* Hoboken, NJ: Howell Book House, 1999.

Lynn A. Hamilton, *Caring for Your Fish.* Weigl Plano, TX: Educational Associates, 2002.

Jango-Cohen, Judith. *Freshwater Fishes (Perfect Pets).* New York City, NY: Benchmark Books, 2002.

Virginia Silverstein, et al., *Fabulous Fish.* Breckenridge, CO: Twenty-first Century Books, 2003.

Web Sites

American Humane Society
www.americanhumane.org/kids/aquarium.htm
This site has kid-friendly tips for setting up and maintaining a tropical fish tank.

Florida Museum of Natural History
www.flmnh.ufl.edu/fish/Kids/kids.htm
This site has lots of information about fish, including how to avoid a shark attack.

Index

Aquarium, 24, 28–29, 30–33

Balance organs, 15
bettas, 28–29, 38–39, 40, 45
blood, 12
bone, 11
brain, 11
breathing, 12, 43

Cartilage, 11
cold-blooded fish, 11
color, 9, 10
conditioning, 43

Ears, 15
echoes, 16
eggs, 19, 21
electricity, 16
eyes, 14, 15

Fins, 8
fishing, 24
food, 17–18, 34, 41–42, 45
    for people, 24
food chain, 24

freshwater fish
    caring for, 26–35
    introduction, 4–24
    investigating, 36–43
    and people, 24
fry, 19–23

Gills, 11, 12, 28

Hearing, 15
heart, 12

Lateral line system, 16
light, 37, 44
live young, 23

Mating, 19, 20
mouth, 12

Nervous system, 10
nests, 19, 21, 45, 38–39

Oxygen, 11, 12, 21, 28

Pollution, 24
predators, 9, 16, 17, 18, 20, 21, 23

prey, 9, 16

Salmon, 13
scales, 9
scavengers, 17, 18
schools, 20
senses, 14–16
Siamese fighting fish, 28–29
skeleton, 11
smell, 15
sound, 15
spawning, 13, 19
sperm, 19
spinal cord, 11
swim bladder, 12
swimming, 17, 44

Teeth, 18
touch, 15
tropical fish, 9, 30–33

Vertebrate, 11
vibrations, 16

Winter, 28